D1158124

DISCARD

Hetty's New Hat

A humorous
farmyard story

This edition first published in 2006 by
Sea-to-Sea Publications
1980 Lookout Drive
North Mankato
Minnesota 56003

Text © Margaret Nash 2004, 2006
Illustration © Martin Impey 2004

Printed in China

Library of Congress Cataloging-in-Publication Data:

Nash, Margaret, 1939-
  Hetty's new hat / by Margaret Nash.
   p. cm. — (Reading corner)
  Summary: When Hetty the hen is showing off her new hat, a wind unexpectedly snatches
it away for a tour of the farm.
  ISBN 1-59771-007-5
  [1. Hats—Fiction. 2. Chickens—Fiction. 3. Winds—Fiction. 4. Domestic animals—Fiction.
5. Farm life—Fiction.] I. Title. II. Series.

PZ7.N1732He 2005
[E]—dc22

                                                        2004063634

9 8 7 6 5 4 3 2

Published by arrangement with the Watts Publishing Group Ltd, London

Series Editor: Jackie Hamley
Series Advisors: Linda Gambrell, Dr. Barrie Wade, Dr. Hilary Minns
Design: Peter Scoulding

READING CORNER

Hetty's New Hat

Written by
Margaret Nash

Illustrated by
Martin Impey

SEA-TO-SEA
Mankato Collingwood London

Margaret Nash

"I work in my study with the help of Tabitha, my cat, who sits on the chair beside me."

Martin Impey

"I work from a studio at the bottom of my garden, where I have lovely views of the countryside."

Hetty had a new hat.

"Oooh!" said the hens, "you DO look good in that hat!"

Hetty went for a walk
in her new hat.

9

Puff! Hetty's new hat
blew off her head!

The hat blew under the gate.

The hat blew across
the fields.

The hat blew past the
scarecrow ...

... and the horses.

The hat blew into the geese.

The hat blew over the pigs.

Then it landed.

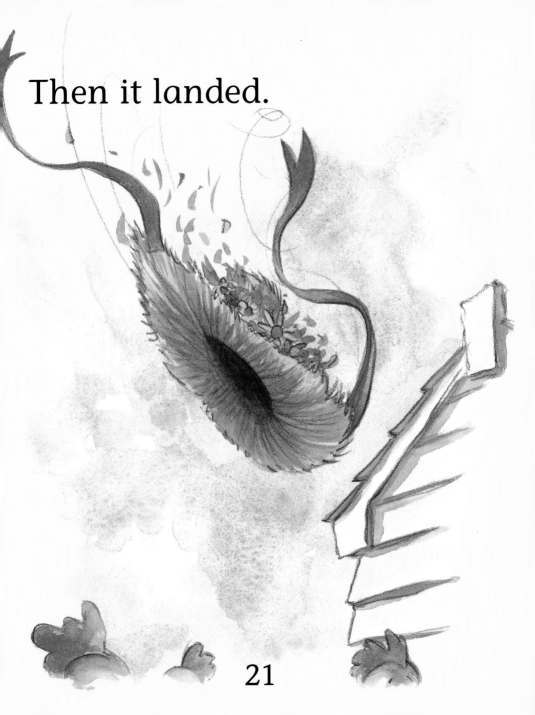

"Oooh!" said the hens, "you DO look good in that hat!"

23

Notes for parents and teachers

READING CORNER has been structured to provide maximum support for new readers. The stories may be used by adults for sharing with young children. Primarily, however, the stories are designed for newly independent readers, whether they are reading these books in bed at night, or in the reading corner at school or in the library.

Starting to read alone can be a daunting prospect. READING CORNER helps by providing visual support and repeating words and phrases, while making reading enjoyable. These books will develop confidence in the new reader, and encourage a love of reading that will last a lifetime!

If you are reading this book with a child, here are a few tips:

1. Make reading fun! Choose a time to read when you and the child are relaxed and have time to share the story.

2. Encourage children to reread the story, and to retell the story in their own words, using the illustrations to remind them what has happened.

3. Give praise! Remember that small mistakes need not always be corrected.

READING CORNER covers three grades of early reading ability, with three levels at each grade. Each level has a certain number of words per story, indicated by the number of bars on the spine of the book, to allow you to choose the right book for a young reader:

GRADE 1	GRADE 2	GRADE 3
50 words	130 words	250 words
70 words	160 words	350 words
100 words	200 words	450 words